Is it BIG or small?

Bobbie Kalman

Crabtree Publishing Company

www.crabtreebooks.com

Created by Bobbie Kalman

Dedicated by Andrea Crabtree
For Charlie, my shining star.

**Author and
Editor-in-Chief**
Bobbie Kalman

Editors
Reagan Miller
Robin Johnson

Photo research
Crystal Sikkens

Production coordinator
Katherine Kantor

Design
Bobbie Kalman
Katherine Kantor
Samantha Crabtree (cover)

Illustrations
Bonna Rouse: page 24

Photographs
All images © Shutterstock.com except:
© iStockphoto.com: page 13 (top)
Digital Stock: page 20 (right)
Digital Vision: pages 6, 8

Library and Archives Canada Cataloguing in Publication

Kalman, Bobbie, 1947-
    Is it big or small? / Bobbie Kalman.

(Looking at nature)
Includes index.
ISBN 978-0-7787-3316-4 (bound).--ISBN 978-0-7787-3336-2 (pbk.)

    1. Size judgment--Juvenile literature. 2. Size perception--Juvenile
literature. 3. Nature--Juvenile literature. I. Title. II. Series: Looking at
nature (St. Catharines, Ont.)

BF299.S5K34 2007   j508   C2007-904235-X

Library of Congress Cataloging-in-Publication Data

Kalman, Bobbie.
    Is it big or small? / Bobbie Kalman.
        p. cm. -- (Looking at nature)
    Includes index.
    ISBN-13: 978-0-7787-3316-4 (rlb)
    ISBN-10: 0-7787-3316-5 (rlb)
    ISBN-13: 978-0-7787-3336-2 (pb)
    ISBN-10: 0-7787-3336-X (pb)
    1. Size perception--Juvenile literature. 2. Size judgment--Juvenile
literature. I. Title. II. Series.

BF299.S5K35 2007
153.7'52--dc22

2007026954

Crabtree Publishing Company

www.crabtreebooks.com   1-800-387-7650

**Published in Canada
Crabtree Publishing**
616 Welland Ave.
St. Catharines, Ontario
L2M 5V6

**Published in the United States
Crabtree Publishing**
PMB16A
350 Fifth Ave., Suite 3308
New York, NY 10118

**Published in the United Kingdom
Crabtree Publishing**
White Cross Mills
High Town, Lancaster
LA1 4XS

**Published in Australia
Crabtree Publishing**
386 Mt. Alexander Rd.
Ascot Vale (Melbourne)
VIC 3032

Contents

Big or small?   4

Huge or tiny?   6

How tall are they?   8

What size are they?   10

Wide or narrow?   12

Heavy or light?   14

Short but heavy   16

More or fewer?   18

High or low?   20

Guess their sizes!   22

Words to know and Index   24

Big or small?

Some things are **big**. Some things are **small**. This mother horse is big. Her **foal**, or baby horse, is small. The mother horse is bigger than the foal. The foal is smaller than its mother.

The dog is smaller
than the foal. The dog
is the smallest of the
three animals. Which
is the biggest animal?

5

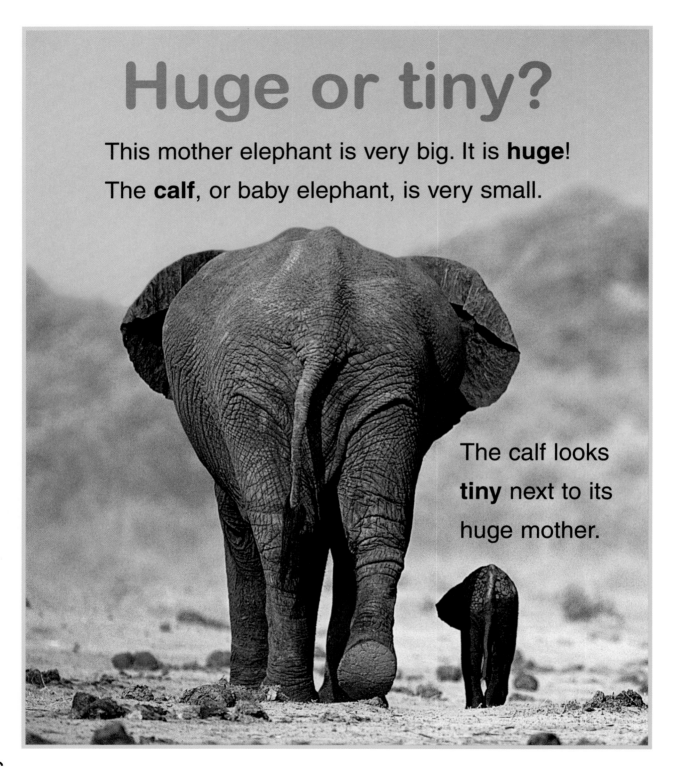

Huge or tiny?

This mother elephant is very big. It is **huge**!

The **calf**, or baby elephant, is very small.

The calf looks **tiny** next to its huge mother.

6

The middle elephant is small, but it is not tiny. The two elephants beside it are bigger, but they are not huge. They are **medium-sized**. All three elephants are still growing. One day, they will be as big as the mother elephant on page 6.

How tall are they?

Giraffes are very **tall** animals. They are not **short**. There are four giraffes in this picture. The giraffe **calf**, or baby, is shorter than the three adult giraffes. One giraffe is taller than the other giraffes. Which is the tallest giraffe?

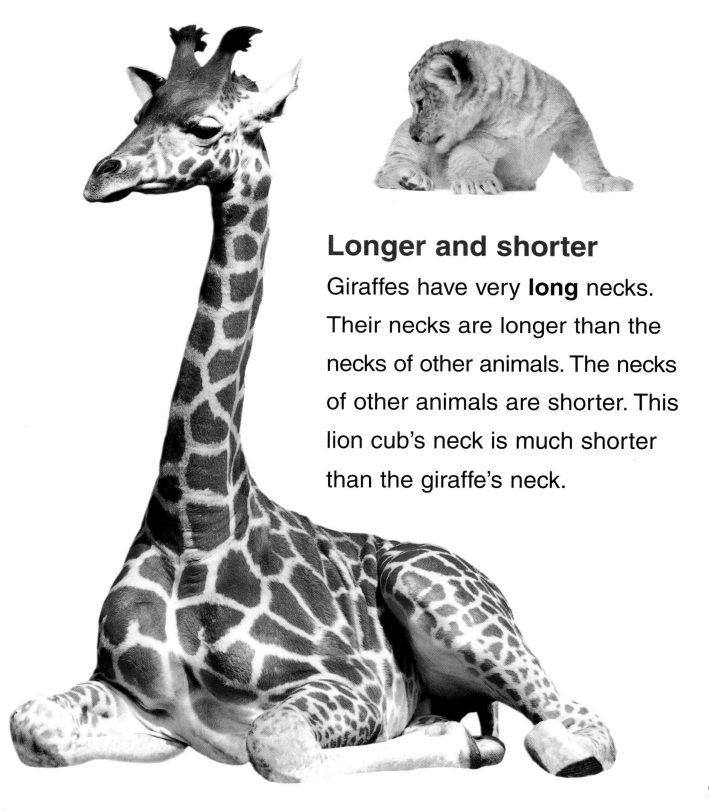

Longer and shorter

Giraffes have very **long** necks. Their necks are longer than the necks of other animals. The necks of other animals are shorter. This lion cub's neck is much shorter than the giraffe's neck.

What size are they?

Baby deer are called **fawns**. These two fawns were born at the same time. They are **twins**. The fawns are smaller than their mother, but one fawn is not bigger than the other fawn. They are both the **same size**.

These four dogs are the same size. Why does the dog on the left look smaller? Look at its legs.

There are two parent lynxes and three baby lynxes in this picture. Which lynxes do you think are the same size?

Wide or narrow?

Some animal bodies are **wide**. Wide is big from side to side. This eagle ray is a kind of fish. It has two large **fins** on its sides. The fins make the ray's body wide.

fin

fin

This fish is an angelfish. An angelfish's body is long from front to back, but it is not wide. The fish's body is **narrow**. Narrow is having little space between one side and the other.

Heavy or light?

This girl has a big dog. She can hold it, but she cannot lift it. The girl cannot carry the dog. The dog is very **heavy**.

This girl has a small dog. She can lift it easily. The dog is not heavy. The dog is **light**. It does not **weigh** very much. Are you lighter or heavier than this little dog?

15

Short but heavy

This pony is short, but it is heavy.

The girl cannot carry the pony. The pony is too heavy. It is heavier than the girl.

The girl is taller than the pony, but she is lighter than the pony. The pony can easily carry the girl. The girl is not as heavy as the pony.

Do you see what I mean?

More or fewer?

More means a bigger number of something. **Fewer** means a smaller number of something. There are kittens and lion cubs on this page. Are there more lion cubs than kittens? Are there fewer lion cubs than kittens?

kittens

lion cubs

How many kittens are on this page? How many bunnies are there? Are there more kittens or more bunnies on this page? How many kittens are on both pages?

bunnies

High or low?

Mountains are tall areas of land. Mountains are **high above** the ground. This girl is standing at the **top** of a mountain. She is high above the ground.

20

These people are at the **bottom** of a big mountain. They are not high above the ground. They are on the ground. They are **lower** than any place on the mountain.

21

Guess their sizes!

Which of these animals is tall?
Which animals are short and
small? Which animal is light?
Which is heavy? Which is long?

butterfly

rhinoceros

emu

snake

emu chicks

Which animal is small?

Which animal is big?

Which animal is wide?

Which animal is narrow?

eagle

butterfly fish

Great Dane

chihuahua

Answers:

Page 22: The emu is tall. The emu chicks are short and small. The butterfly is light. The rhinoceros is heavy. The snake is long. Page 23: A chihuahua is small. A Great Dane is big. An eagle's wings are wide. A butterfly fish's body is narrow.

23

Words to know and Index

big pages 4, 5, 6, 7, 10, 12, 14, 18, 21, 23
huge pages 6, 7

fewer page 18

heavy pages 14, 15, 16, 17, 22, 23

light pages 14, 15, 17, 22, 23

more pages 18, 19

narrow pages 12, 13, 23

short pages 8, 9, 16, 22, 23

small pages 4, 5, 6, 7, 10, 11, 15, 18, 22, 23
tiny pages 6, 7

tall pages 8, 17, 20, 22, 23

wide pages 12, 13, 23

Other index words

bottom page 21
long pages 9, 13, 22, 23
medium-sized page 7
same size pages 10-11
top page 20

Printed in the U.S.A.